How to Ward Off Wolves

How to Ward Off Wolves

Catherine Leblanc  Roland Garrigue

INSIGHT KIDS

San Rafael, California

Wolves

come out only at night.
You'll see their yellow eyes
peering out of the darkness.

Don't think for a minute
that they're stronger than you.
You can ward them off!
Be brave!

If you hide under a sheet,
the wolves will take you for a GHOST
and run for the woods!

You can sleep hanging upside down.
The wolves will think you're a bat,
definitely not their favorite snack!

You can call for your MOM! so loud and so long
that the wolves will leave disgusted—
they hate to be disturbed.

You can blow on wolves
to RUFFLE and FLUFF their fur
until they float away.

You can dazzle them by turning on all the lights
and adding some garlands and ribbons and wrappings.
Turn your wolf into a Christmas tree!

You can crank up the music
and carol and sing;
that really makes wolves steam!
You can dance on your bed;
they'll try to copy you
and slip and fall on the rug!

You can suck on hard candy...

and then spit it out!
The wolves will howl and growl and run.

You also can warn the wolves
that your dad is right behind you
—and he's got his hunting rifle!

You can also try some big bad words.
Impressed by your nerve,
they'll slink off.

You can tell them a scary story
that will make them really TREMBLE,
a story about children who go hunting.

You can make them believe that for dinner
you'll bake a pie of mashed up wolves.

Or send them next door
to visit your little sister;
she's much tastier to eat!

And, of course, you can play with the wolves.
Pretend to be a wolf yourself or try hide-and-seek.
Three, two, one! Ready or not, here I come!

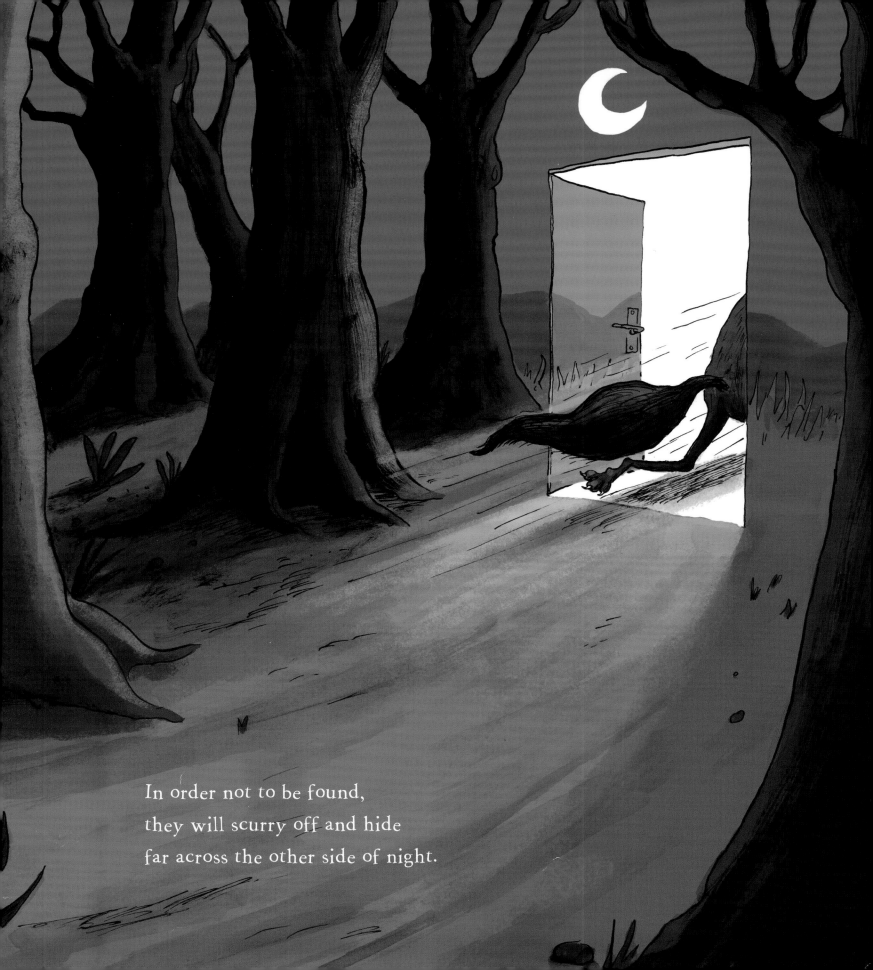

In order not to be found,
they will scurry off and hide
far across the other side of night.

Go ahead!

Look under your bed.
No more big grey wolf—
just a smelly old sock!

But what is that glowing
over there in the dark?
It's the eyes of a little wolf pup,
who is listening and wondering
how the story will end . . .

The End

For Annie, who knows wolves well, and for Louane, her
great-granddaughter, who is just discovering them.
—CL

For my sister Gabrielle, my brothers John and Pierre . . .
my pack of wolves!
—RG

INSIGHT
KIDS

PO Box 3088
San Rafael, CA 94912
www.insighteditions.com

Find us on Facebook: www.facebook.com/InsightEditions
Follow us on Twitter: @insighteditions

First published in the United States in 2013 by Insight Editions.
Originally published in France in 2008 by Éditions Glénat.
Comment Ratatiner les Loups?
by C. Leblanc and R. Garrigue © 2008 Éditions Glénat
Translation © 2013 Insight Editions

Thanks to Christopher Goff and Marie Goff-Tuttle
for their help in translating this book.

Library of Congress Cataloging-in-Publication Data available.

5373

ISBN: 978-1-60887-194-0

ROOTS of PEACE   🌳 REPLANTED PAPER

Insight Editions, in association with Roots of Peace, will plant two trees for each
tree used in the manufacturing of this book. Roots of Peace is an internationally
renowned humanitarian organization dedicated to eradicating land mines worldwide
and converting war-torn lands into productive farms and wildlife habitats. Roots of
Peace will plant two million fruit and nut trees in Afghanistan and provide farmers
there with the skills and support necessary for sustainable land use.

Manufactured in China by Insight Editions

10 9 8 7 6 5 4 3 2 1